Jeff Jarka

Love That Kitty!

The Story of a Boy Who Wanted to Be a Cat

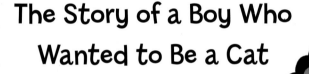

Henry Holt and Company • New York

Peter was an ordinary boy, almost.

Then, one day, Peter decided to become a cat.

Not everyone thought this was a good idea.

But Peter was happy.

PURRRRRRRRRRRRRRRRRRR

Peter was good at being a kitty. He loved to take catnaps and soon mastered the art of purring.

Peter practiced
his balance . . .

He could sneak
without a sound . . .

. . . and pounce on hapless, unsuspecting prey.

Peter even learned how to be invisible!

But he also knew how to attract attention.

Peter discovered the joy of yarn.

He practiced
good grooming . . .

. . . and good hygiene.

But while Peter was very good at being a cat,
he was not always a good cat.

He scratched the furniture.

He became an expert climber.

Peter refused to take baths.

He even learned how to shed.

Then, one day, Peter decided to become a boy again.

Peter's parents were very happy . . .

For Benjamin and Jonah

Henry Holt and Company, LLC
Publishers since 1866
175 Fifth Avenue
New York, New York 10010
www.HenryHoltKids.com

Henry Holt® is a registered trademark of Henry Holt and Company, LLC.
Copyright © 2010 by Jeff Jarka
All rights reserved.
Distributed in Canada by H. B. Fenn and Company Ltd.

Library of Congress Cataloging-in-Publication Data
Jarka, Jeff.
Love that kitty : the story of a boy who wanted to be a cat / Jeff Jarka. — 1st ed.
p. cm.
Summary: Tired of being an ordinary boy, Peter decides to become a cat.
ISBN 978-0-8050-9053-6
[1. Cats—Fiction.] I. Title.
PZ7.J285Ln 2010
[E]—dc22
2009027411

First Edition—2010
The artist used Adobe® Photoshop® to create the illustrations for this book.
Printed in June 2010 in China by Macmillan Production (Asia) Ltd., Kwun Tong, Kowloon, Hong Kong, on acid-free paper.∞
Supplier Code: 10

1 3 5 7 9 10 8 6 4 2